Kerin Finds Her Beat

Written by

Shanequa Waison-Rattray

Illustrated by DG

Published by Shanequa Waison-Rattray
Baltimore, MD

Library of Congress Control Number: 2020910323

ISBN-13: 978-0-578-70599-6

Special Acknowledgments

Thank you, God! To my loves, Paul, Jaelyn, and Gavin, thank you for pushing me to be the better me each day! To my family and my circle—thank you for being supportive and motivating!

Chapter 1

I stood in front of the mirror with my new dance uniform on. I had told my mother that I wanted to start dance class, but now I was so nervous! I hoped I'd do ok. It was my first day of ballet.

I love to see ballerinas dance so gracefully. I looked at the poster on my wall. "I want to dance just like you," I said to the model in the picture. I looked down at my leotard, tights, and pink dance shoes and then back at the mirror. Then I heard my mom call me, alerting me that it was time to go to class, but then scurried back to the mirror. "I can do this; I just need to be brave!" I said as I grabbed my dance bag and headed out the door.

On the ride to dance class, I wondered to myself, "What if I fall? What if the other kids laugh at me? Will there be ballerinas there?" I sighed as I looked out the window. I watched different cars drive past, and the sunlight grazed my face. Not even my favorite song on the radio took me out of my trance.

After a few lights and turns, we arrived at the dance academy. "We're here. Are you ready?" my mom asked while turning to face me.

"I guess," I said shyly as I gazed down at my hands.

"It's ok to be nervous, Kerin," my mother said. "Everyone gets nervous when trying something new. You will be just fine!"

"Ok," I mumbled and unfastened my seat belt. We walked across the parking lot. I held my mother's hand tightly as I saw girls coming in and out of the dance school, all dressed in their dance uniforms.

We arrived at the front desk, and I looked around. There were pictures of different students posing in costumes on the wall. I could hear my mom speaking to the receptionist, and I peeked around her arm to see what was going on in the studio. Everyone had on their dance uniforms. Some were tall, some were short, but all dressed alike.

Just then, one of the instructors came up to my mom and me. "Hi, my name is Ms. Patricia. I am one of the dance instructors here. What is your name?" She extended her hand to me.

Ohh, she is talking to me, I said in my head. "I'm Kerin," I said quietly.

"She is a lil' nervous today," my mom stated as she rubbed my hand for reassurance, and I felt comforted.

"No need to be nervous. You will have a good time. Come on, I will show you around the school," Ms. Patricia said.

Chapter 2

We all began to tour the school. We walked into the first dance studio, which some girls were leaving. "This is our tap and jazz studio," Ms. Patricia said.

I peeked in and saw that the girls were lined up. The instructor was giving the dancers directions. My eyes grew in excitement as the music came on and the girls began their routine.

"Do you like what you see so far?" my mom asked as she looked down at me, noticing my excitement.

Yes! I nodded my head in delight.

"So here we have our ballet room." Ms. Patricia pointed to the next room. "This is our advanced class with some of our older girls." Soothing music played as the girls moved in sync.

"This is amazing!" I said as the dancers glided across the studio.

We continued our tour and came to the studio where my class was held. "Ok, Kerin, you can put your things over in the cubbies before your class begins," Ms. Patricia said as she pointed to the corner in the studio. "Your instructor's name is Mrs. Donna. She will be in shortly."

My mom and I walked over to the cubby section, where she helped me place my things in a cubby. "Once class is over, I will be right outside waiting for you," my mom said. "You will be just fine." She smiled warmly and gave me a quick hug.

I stood to the side as some girls started walking in. They walked toward the cubbies to place their belongings there. As they passed me, they stared and whispered. I looked down to my feet. *I wonder what they are saying*, I thought to myself.

"Hi, I'm Nia. What is your name?" a girl asked me. She was about my height and had a tooth missing.

"I'm Kerin!"

"Oh, you are new here!" she continued, putting her things away in the cubby. "We have to sit over there until Mrs. Donna comes in. Come on, I will show you." Nia pointed and walked over to the middle of the class.

Chapter 3

There was a group of girls that were all talking when we arrived. We sat down, and everyone looked at me. "This is Kerin," Nia said to everyone. "She is new here."

Shock took over me. I didn't know what to say.

"Hiiii!" the girls all said in unison.

"Hi," I said shyly.

"Have you danced before?" Lillian, a girl with glasses, asked.

"Nope, this is my first time," I answered.

"How old are you?" another asked.

"I'm seven!"

"Oh, I'm seven, too!"

"I'm eight!" one of the other girls said.

Everyone was talking at the same time, and I sat and took in the atmosphere. There were three rows of dance bars in the room. There also was a large mirror that reached from the ceiling to the floor. A TV and speakers were mounted on the wall.

As I was taking in the surroundings, Mrs. Donna came into the room. "Good afternoon, ladies," she said as she walked in with her dance bag hanging from her shoulder.

"Good afternoon, Mrs. Donna!" all the girls sang. Then they all stood up.

"Come on," Nia whispered, "you can stand next to me."

I smiled as I followed her to the dance bar.

"How is everyone doing today?" the instructor asked. "Ready to get started?"

"Yes, Mrs. Donna!"

She walked to the middle of the class and looked around. "Oh, hello. You must be Kerin." She looked at me and smiled. I waved and smiled back. "Is this your first ballet class?" Mrs. Donna asked as she walked over and stood next to me.

"Yes," I answered as I looked up at her.

"Your very first dance class *ever*?!" she asked as she smiled and placed her hands on her hips.

"Yesss!" I giggled as everyone in the class laughed.

"Well, it's a pleasure to have you here, Kerin! We will have fun, and you will learn a lot." She turned to the rest of the class. "Everyone, let's say hello to Kerin! This is her first day of ballet," Mrs. Donna announced.

"Hi Kerin!" everyone said. I smiled and waved hello.

"I'm going to have you stand right here, ok?" Mrs. Donna placed me at one of the dance bars. "I will stand in the front, and you, along with the rest of the class, will follow my lead. If you have any questions or need to stop, you just let me know, ok?"

"Ok!" I replied and looked around at the other girls. They had all put one hand on the bar, and I did the same.

Music was flowing out from the speakers. It was soft and soothing. I couldn't believe that I was actually in a ballet class.

Mrs. Donna was showing the class different positions. "Ok class, let's get in first position," Mrs. Donna instructed, and demonstrated. All the girls followed, and I looked at Mrs. Donna to see how she positioned her feet. I did exactly what she was showing us and glanced around to see if I looked the same as the rest of the class.

"Next, second position." She clapped her hands and walked around the class. "And third position," she said. By that time, Mrs. Donna had come back to me and assisted me to make sure I was doing the position correctly. "Good job, Kerin!"

"Thank you," I whispered as she continued to walk around the class. She clapped her hands to the beat of the music as we continued to practice the different positions that we were taught.

Eventually, the music stopped, and everyone relaxed their posture. "Ladies, make sure that you practice your positions at home. We will be learning more positions to add next class," Mrs. Donna said, as this was the end of class.

"Ok, Mrs. Donna!" everyone said in unison.

"See you next class!" Mrs. Donna waved as everyone went to the cubbies to prepare to leave.

"Kerin, you did a really good job today! Did you enjoy class?" Mrs. Donna stood next to me, smiling.

"I did. I really liked it!" I answered as I smiled and started to put my clothes on.

As I walked out, I easily spotted my mom. I was excited to tell her about my first day of ballet. "Hi, Mom!" I said as I hugged her.

"Hi, sweet pea! How was class?" she asked as she hugged me back.

"I really liked it, and I met a few new friends!" I said excitedly. We started walking outside to the car.

"Oh, that's great! Did you learn anything cool today?"

"Yes, Mrs. Donna taught us different movements and positions. She also told us to practice at home," I answered as I got in the car and put on my seat belt.

"That sounds great. I'm so happy that you liked it," my mom said as she pulled out of the parking lot. "Practice makes perfect, and you will get more comfortable as you go."

"I can't wait," I said. I was so excited, thinking about the next class.

Chapter 4

It was Wednesday afternoon, and I was in my room. I had just finished my homework and wanted to practice for ballet class the next day. My mom was able to find the music that Mrs. Donna used in class. I pressed play, and the music came through the speaker. I stood in front of my mirror in position.

"Ok, Kerin," I said to myself, "what was the first position?" I stood in first position with my heels touching each other and arms out. I lost my balance and fell on the floor. "Ahh, man," I said as I stood and regained my balance. "Let me try this again."

I got into position again. This time, I was able to hold first position. I moved on to second position, my legs separated and arms extended. "Yes!" I got excited as I moved on to the next position.

"Oh no! How are my arms supposed to go? Are they both supposed to be up, or just one?" I looked at myself in the mirror, confused, trying to remember third position. "I got this. Let me just start over." I walked over to the music player and started it over. I got in position, and the music played again.

"Ok, first position." I began to go through the positions again. When I got to third position, the same thing happened. "Why can't I remember this?" I motioned my arms, starting from first position to third. Then it clicked!

"Yes!!" I exclaimed. "I got it!" I moved on to the remaining positions.

My mother peeked in my room to check on me. "Hey, sweet pea! What are you up to?"

"I'm going over my ballet positions. I want to be ready for the next class," I answered as I turned to face her.

"That's great! How is that coming along?"

"It's ok. At first, I couldn't remember a few positions and how my arms were supposed to go, but I finally remembered!" I exclaimed.

"I'm happy for you. Practice makes perfect," my mom said as she smiled and left me to practice.

I went over the positions a few more times before I turned the music off. I lay on the rug, looking at the poster on my wall of my favorite ballet dancer. "I will be great like you one day."

"Kerin, it's time for dinner," my mother called from downstairs.

"Ok Mom, I'm coming." I jumped up and ran out of my room. Then I doubled back and winked at myself in the mirror. "You got this!" I said and then ran downstairs for dinner.

Chapter 5

It was recess time at school, and some of my friends and I were sitting by the swings talking. Laila was jumping rope, I was sitting on the tire swing, and Justine was sitting on the bench. "I started karate last week," Justine said. "It's pretty cool!"

"Really?" Laila and I exclaimed together.

"Yes. I didn't think I would like it, but after some classes, I actually like going," she answered.

"Wow! And I'm excited about swim class," Laila said as she began to jump with her rope.

I was swinging around in the tire as the wind blew through my ponytails. "I started dance class this week," I said as I spun around and around.

"That is so cool, Kerin!" said Laila.

"What kind of dance class?" Justine said at the same time.

I stopped swinging to face them. "It's ballet," I said shyly.

"Do you get to wear a tutu?" Laila asked excitedly.

"No, I wear a leotard and tights with ballet shoes," I answered as I sat on the bench next to Justine.

"I wish I could take dance class," Justine said. "Do you like it?"

"It's still new, and I was so nervous during the first class," I answered. "I have a lot of practicing to do."

"Can you show us some moves?" Laila asked.

"Yeah, show us something that you learned," Justine added.

"Uhhhh, I don't know. I'm still learning," I answered, feeling bashful.

"Oh, come on Kerin, just show us one move," Justine said.

Just then, the school bell rang, letting us know it was the end of recess. I felt relief come over me. I really didn't want to show my friends any moves. I wasn't ready and needed a lot more practice. "Race you to the line!" I tagged each of them and took off running to the school building.

Chapter 6

"And one, two, three, four. One, two, three, four." Mrs. Donna snapped her fingers as the class practiced each position. I was in the front row, making sure to keep up with each position and the class. "Good job, ladies!" The music stopped, and so did everyone.

"Ok ladies, we are going to do circle time." The girls started to sit in a circle.

I looked around and moved slowly, not sure what was about to happen. I sat next to Nia and asked, "What is circle time?"

She leaned over to whisper in my ear. "It's when Mrs. Donna chooses one girl to dance in the middle to see if we are learning our positions."

"Ohhhhh!" I exclaimed. "I don't want to be chosen to do that."

"Kerin, you will be ok! It's how we learn and do better," Nia told me.

"Have you ever been in the middle?" I asked as I saw Mrs. Donna starting to walk around.

"Yes, plenty of times."

The music came on, and Mrs. Donna was still walking around the circle. "Ok, Gabby, you are up!" I sighed with relief as Gabby stood and got in position in the middle of the circle. "Are you ready?" Mrs. Donna asked Gabby.

"Yes, Mrs. Donna."

"Ok, let's begin." Mrs. Donna started calling positions as Gabby breezed through the movements. When she was finished, Mrs.

Donna praised her for doing a good job, and Gabby sat back in her seat.

"Ok, let's see who is next," Mrs. Donna sang and walked around the circle. "Hmmmm." She tapped her chin, and all the girls giggled as I prayed not to be chosen. "Nia, you're up!"

Another sigh of relief as I looked over to Nia. She got right up and got into first position. I gave her a smile of encouragement as the music began to play. Nia started to do her movements as Mrs. Donna snapped her fingers and called them out. I was excited for my new friend, and I thought she was doing a great job.

"Very good!" Mrs. Donna said. "Ok, ladies. At our next class, we will incorporate more movements with our positions. We have a show in a few months, so we must practice, practice, practice."

We all stood. Many girls were departing to their next class, and others were leaving for the day. I was putting on my sweater as I walked over to Nia.

"Hey Nia, you did a really good job!" I exclaimed.

"Thanks, Kerin!"

"Were you nervous?"

"Umm, a little, but it went away. You'll see if Mrs. Donna chooses you one day."

"Yeah, I guess. I will see you next class." I waved. "Bye!"

Nia waved back as we walked out of class together.

I need to make sure I practice, I thought to myself. *I need to nail these positions, and now we have a show coming up. Oh my! I have work to do.*

I walked out the front of the dance studio to my mother, who was waiting. "Hi, Kerin. Was class good?"

"Yes. I have a lot of work to do, though," I said as we walked to the parking lot.

"Oh, ok." She gave a little giggle.

"Mrs. Donna said we will start practicing for a show, and we have to practice, practice, practice!" I told her as I got in the car and fastened my seat belt. "And now we have something called circle time."

"Really? What is that?" my mother asked as we began to drive off.

"We have to stand in the middle of the circle by ourselves and do the positions that we learned in class! Like, everyone is looking at you!" My eyes got big as I explained what had happened during today's class.

"Sounds interesting. Were you chosen today?"

"No, thank goodness! I would have been so nervous, Mom."

"Ok, ok!" she said. "I'm sure you would have done just fine. You just have to keep practicing, because practice makes..."

"Perfect." I finished her sentence.

She winked at me through the mirror. "How about we get a milkshake to cool off those legs from all that dancing?"

"Sounds like a great idea, because I will be using them a lot!"

Chapter 7

A few classes came and went, and I practiced over and over. We were getting close to our first performance, and my excitement was growing each day!

I was sitting on my porch, waiting to go to dance class. It was a nice day outside, but for some reason, I was feeling a little down. I heard the door behind me open and knew that it was my mother.

She greeted me as she sat next to me. "Hey, Kerin!"

"Hi, Mom," I said as I looked up to acknowledge her.

"Ah, sweet pea, why so sad?" she asked as she nudged my shoulder.

"Have you ever felt like you couldn't do anything?" I asked my mother. "We have our performance coming up, and I'm super nervous." I cupped my face with my hands.

My mom turned to me to answer. "Well, what makes you nervous? You have been doing very well in dance. You've been practicing, and I see the progress. Mrs. Donna has even said that she is proud of you."

"I guess," I said. "But what if I mess up? Some of the other girls are really good, and I'm nowhere close to being as good as them—"

"Whoa, whoa, slow down there," my mother cut in. "Kerin, people mess up all the time. The more you practice, the better you will get." She raised my chin so I would look at her. "You will be just fine. You have to believe in yourself and that you will do great. I believe in you!" She smiled, and I smiled back at her and gave her a hug.

"Thanks, Mom!"

"You're welcome! Now let's get out of here before you're late for class."

Chapter 8

"Hi, Kerin!" Nia said as she set her bag next to me to get ready for class.

"Hey Nia, how are you?" I replied, putting on my ballet shoes.

"I'm doing good! Are you ready for class today? I'm so excited for the recital coming up!"

"You are?" I asked, looking at her.

"Yes! We get to show our family all of the work we have done so far. Aren't you excited?"

"Uhh, I guess," I answered. "I'm a little nervous."

"For my first recital, I was nervous also. It goes away, though." We got up and prepared for class.

"Good afternoon, class," Mrs. Donna said. We all greeted her in unison.

"We have our first recital just around the corner, so we will go over a lot today. Let's get in position."

We all followed directions as the music began to play. We began with a warm-up and then went straight to our recital routine.

"Ladies, make sure you extend your arms and point those toes," Mrs. Donna instructed. "Kerin, straighten your back," she said as she walked past me, and I straightened my back.

I worked really hard and stayed focused as I remembered each part of the routine. We practiced what seems like a hundred times during class that day. I was exhausted!

After class, we all were preparing to leave. "Wow, that was a lot," one of my classmates said. "I'm sweating!"

Everyone in the group chuckled.

"We did the routine a lot," Nia said as she put on her shoes.

"Yeah, 'practice makes perfect' is what my mom says," I replied, putting on my sweater.

"I can't wait until the recital so we can be on stage with our costumes," Lillian said, adjusting her glasses.

We all exited the dance studio, and I spotted my mom at the front desk. "Hi Mom," I said, and then noticed she was carrying a bag.

"Hey Kerin, I have your costume!" she said excitedly. "I can't wait to see it on you."

"Me either!" I said as I tried to peek through the small window on the garment bag.

"Hey, hey, we will look when we get home." She tried to hide the bag from me as we shared a laugh. We said goodnight to everyone and headed home.

Chapter 9

I couldn't have moved any faster as I headed straight to my room. "Mom, you're moving too slow!" I called out from my room.

"I'm coming, I'm coming. I don't have the energy of an eight-year-old, you know," she said as she climbed the stairs.

I laughed as I began to strip off my clothes, so excited to finally see my costume.

"Ok, I'm here." My mom came in and placed the garment bag in the closet. She began to unzip the bag as I stood with big eyes, trying to hold my excitement.

"Ohhh, wow," she exclaimed, "this is beautiful!"

I stood next to my mom as I reached out to feel the fabric. "Oh my goodness. This is amazing!" I shouted. "Can I try it on now? Look, it has glitter, and it's so soft."

"Whew, someone is really excited! Ok, you can try it on, I guess," my mom teased as she began to remove the costume from the hanger. "Ok, be careful so we don't mess it up." She assisted me with putting on the costume.

When I was all zipped up, I stood in front my of mirror in awe. I couldn't believe how beautiful I was in the costume. I twirled around and saw how the skirt moved so swiftly.

"You look gorgeous, Kerin!" my mom said, covering her mouth.

"Thank you!" I said, smiling as I turned around some more. Then I stopped. "Mom! Are you going to cry?" I asked with one hand on my hip.

"Noooo, you look so cute!" she said, wiping her eyes as she came to hug me.

"Oh Mom," I laughed, "please tell me that you won't cry at the recital."

"I can't say that I will or I won't"—she placed her hand on her chest—"but I'm so excited for you." We both looked in the mirror. "Now let's take this off before it gets messed up!"

"Aww, just a few more minutes. Pleeeassse?!" I asked with my hands clasped.

"Ok, just a few minutes. I will go start dinner," she said as she headed out.

I danced, swayed, and twirled around my room in my costume. I looked at the poster on my wall and copied the pose. "I got this!" I said as I danced some more.

Chapter 10

It was a bright Saturday morning. My alarm went off, and I groaned and turned over. "It's too early," I thought to myself as I put the blanket over my head.

As I had just gotten comfortable, the alarm sounded again. My eyes shot open. "It's recital day!" I exclaimed as I jumped out of the bed. I opened my bedroom door and ran downstairs to the kitchen.

"Good morning," I said as I sat at the table.

"Good morning, superstar!" my dad said as he passed me to sit down.

"Good morning, Dad," I giggled, fixing myself some of my favorite cereal.

"You ready for today to show us what you got?"

"As ready as I can be."

"Well, I can't wait to see you on stage today. I'm so excited!" my mom said, walking in with my baby brother. "Let's eat up so we can start preparing for today."

I smiled as I ate my breakfast.

My mother combed and brushed my hair into a bun, and I got dressed and was ready to go. "We are leaving in five minutes," Mom said as she went out of my room.

I got my dance bag and made sure all of my things were in there. Then I walked up to my mirror and examined myself. "Recital day is here!" I said to myself. I put my bag over my shoulder and began to walk out of my room. Then I walked back up to my mirror and said, "You got this!"

When we arrived at the auditorium, there were people everywhere! Some were laughing, some were moving fast through the hallways. There were also many families. I held onto my dance bag and followed my mother to the dancers' assigned area.

We arrived at the desk. "Hi Kerin, how are you?" Ms. Patricia asked in greeting as she handed me a name tag.

"I'm doing fine," I answered with a smile.

"Well, you look gorgeous! Are you ready for your recital?" she asked.

"As ready as I'm going to be." I smiled and looked at my mom. She gave me a friendly nudge as we went into the area for the dancers.

We looked around to find Mrs. Donna. She waved at us as we walked over to her. "Hey, Kerin." She hugged me. "We will get set up here. You can hang your costume over here," she told my mom and me as we followed her.

"Mom, we will be getting dressed soon for showtime," Mrs. Donna told my mother.

"Ok that sounds great," my mom answered as she sat next to me. "Ok sweet pea, this is it! I'm not going to ask if you are ready. I know you are," she said, looking at me. I felt relief as she held my hand.

"I am ready and excited," I said. "Maybe a little nervous."

"And that is just fine. When you hit the stage, all of that will go away, and you'll give it all that you have," she said, smiling down at me.

"Really?"

"I promise!" she said as she kissed my forehead.

Some of the instructors were making announcements. "I think that's my cue. I'm going to go get a good seat in the audience and take a lot of pics," my mother gushed.

"Oh, Mom!" I blushed and began walking to where all my classmates were.

"I will see you soon," my mother called out.

I saw Nia with her mother and gave her a wave. She smiled and waved back to me as she walked over. "Hey Kerin, are you ready for your first show?" she asked.

"Yeah, I guess. I think I will be more ready once we get dressed," I answered as we sat in our section.

"The costume is so cool. I can't wait!" she exclaimed.

"Yeah. When I tried it on, I didn't want to take it off." We both smiled.

"And now we get to show everyone our pretty costumes and our routine," I said.

"Yes, I'm so ready!" Nia exclaimed as she clapped her hands.

Mrs. Donna walked over towards us. "Ok ladies, this is the moment that we've been waiting for. We are going to show everyone how hard we have been working, right?" she asked.

"Right!" we all replied in unison.

"All right, follow me, and we will get dressed and prepare to take the stage." She gave directions, and we followed.

I could hear cheering and clapping on the other side of the curtain. I was standing in position and could feel my heart beating through my chest. My palms were sweating, and I had flutters in my stomach. I could see Mrs. Donna on the other side of the stage ready to give us the cue to go when the music began. I closed my eyes and took a deep breath. "You got this, Kerin; you got this."

The music began, and my eyes shot open. The curtain rose, and the lights shined on us. It was showtime!

Chapter 11

It was an overwhelming feeling. I felt so excited and full of energy. I had just finished my first recital. We exited the stage, and Mrs. Donna was there to give us a group hug. During the embrace, she said, "You all did amazing! I'm so proud of each and every one of you." We all giggled, and some laughed as we were in our huddle.

"We did it!" I hugged Nia.

"Yes, we did. I told you that you would do great," she said as we twirled together.

"It was so exciting," I said as we giggled.

"Ok ladies, let's go find our families." Mrs. Donna escorted us out to the area where we had first met to get dressed, and we started packing our things.

As I was sitting and putting on my pants, I saw my mother walking towards me. I jumped up in excitement and ran into her arms. She embraced me, and it felt so good to feel her warmth. "You did it, kid!" She hugged me tight and kissed my forehead. "I'm so proud of you."

"Thanks, Mom!" I smiled up at her.

We walked back to my seat, and she sat next to me. She helped me pack my costume, and I could overhear her speaking with other parents about the recital. Everyone was excited!

"I took so many pictures," my mom said as she scrolled through her phone. "You looked so cute!"

"Mom!" I giggled.

"I couldn't help it," she laughed as we began walking out the room.

There were so many people in the auditorium's hallway. I held onto my mother's hand as we passed through the crowd of people. I spotted my dad and little brother off to the side. "There goes the superstar!" my dad said in praise as he engulfed me in a hug. "I'm so proud of you."

"Thanks, Dad!" I exclaimed. I felt a tug at my jacket; it was my brother, Amir. "These are for you," he said as he handed me flowers.

I bent down and gave him a hug and kiss on the cheek. "Thank you so much!"

"So how do you feel?" my dad asked.

"Ummmm, I feel ok. I was so nervous backstage, but it went away."

"Well, you did amazing!"

"Thanks, Dad." I blushed.

"Well, let's go celebrate this occasion," my mom said as she clapped her hands and reached for my hand, and we walked outside.

I waved to a few of my classmates as they were posing for pictures and talking with their families. It was a beautiful afternoon, and the sun was shining down on us. "Mom, you were right," I said as we walked down the stairs.

"About what, Kerin?" she asked.

"You told me that if I keep working at learning ballet, I would get better at it. Practice makes perfect!"

"Yep, and now look: You tackled it and made an accomplishment!" she said as she twirled me around in a circle.

I giggled. "Yep, if I can keep at it, be positive, and have patience, I can accomplish anything!"

My mom winked, and we were off to celebrate!

About the Author

Shanequa Waison-Rattray is a wife, a mother of two, and a graduate of Coppin State University in Baltimore, MD. Since she was a little girl, she has always loved reading books. While in middle school, her love of reading increased, as she was able to read books and see the theater plays associated with them. Since then, she has wanted to write books of her own. Rattray loves watching her children read and seeing the excitement that they get from it. Because of this, she wants to share her passion for reading with not only her own children but others, also.

CPSIA information can be obtained
at www.ICGtesting.com
Printed in the USA
LVHW071348100621
689633LV00006B/23

9 780578 705996